Be careful what you and your dragon wish for!

"Who am I going to saw in half?" I say out loud.

Dragon looks up from counting the bags of chocolate chips. "I'm too muscular to saw in half," he says, and flexes his arms. I don't notice any muscles.

Out of the corner of my eye I see my dad walking by in the hallway.

"Dad!" I shout as I run over to him. He stops walking and glances down at me. "Can I practice sawing you in half for the magic show?"

"Uh," he stammers, "I have to help with the baking." Dad rushes to the kitchen.

If no one helps me practice, I won't have a good enough show to earn money for the toy charity and the volcano building kit. I need help. I need a miracle.

Other Books You May Enjoy

WARREN & Dragon

Volcano Deluxe

by Ariel Bernstein

illustrated by Mike Malbrough

PUFFIN BOOKS

PUFFIN BOOKS

An imprint of Penguin Random House LLC, New York

First published in the United States of America by Viking,
an imprint of Penguin Random House, LLC, 2019
Published by Puffin Books, an imprint of Penguin Random House LLC, 2019

Visit us online at penguinrandomhouse.com

LIBRARY OF CONGRESS CATALOGING-IN-PUBLICATION DATA IS AVAILABLE

Puffin Books ISBN 9780451481047

Printed in U.S.A.

1   3   5   7   9   10   8   6   4   2

✖ ✖ ✖

For Debi, the original Ellie—A.B.

For Abe. May you get all
the toys of your dreams. —M.M.

✖ ✖ ✖

CONTENTS

1

The Meaning of Life

I, Warren Reginald Nesbitt, at only seven years of age, have discovered the meaning of life. Okay, not of *all* life. But I've discovered the meaning of *my* life. Because the most amazing thing ever is staring me in the face right in the middle of Tony's Tops Toy Store. The meaning of my life is that I have to have the Deluxe Volcano Building Set Supreme.

Dragon, my pet dragon, has the same exact thought. "I need this more than I've ever needed anything in my whole entire existence," he declares as he stands next to me, staring at the same box. Dragon's lived a couple hundred years longer than me, so that's saying something.

The Deluxe Volcano Building Set Supreme is practically calling our names.

"It says the lava can shoot up to three feet in the air," I read from the bright orange and red box.

Dragon wipes his mouth with a claw. "I think I'm drooling," he says.

I check my mouth. No drool yet.

"Warren!" I hear my mom call. I twist my head to see her marching up the aisle. "So, have you found something?" she asks.

Dragon points to the box. "Please, can we get it?" he asks her as he jumps up and down. "If you buy this for me, I promise to never cause the smoke detectors to go off again in the middle of the night. I promise to share it with Warren. Sometimes. Maybe. And I promise to not eat all the marshmallows as soon as you bring them home from the supermarket!"

I notice that Dragon crosses his claws at that

last promise. It doesn't matter though. Mom just ignores Dragon, because she doesn't understand that Dragon is real. No one but me hears Dragon talk or sees him move. They think he's a stuffed animal.

Now it's my turn to point to the box holding the volcano building set. "Can I get this, Mom? Please?" I put on my best pleading face.

"Warren, you're supposed to be looking for a toy for Avik's birthday," she says, shaking her head.

"Can I get Avik a toy *and* get this for me?" I ask.

Mom shakes her head again. I wonder if she ever gets dizzy doing that.

"Well, can we get the volcano building set for Avik?" I ask, already devising a plan to trade Avik the volcano building set for something else.

Mom checks the price tag and grimaces. "It's a little much," she says. "Sorry, Warren. There are less expensive volcano building sets here." Mom motions to a few other boxes underneath the deluxe version.

I inspect the less expensive volcano building toys. "Mom, these volcanos only have lava fall out the side of the volcano. They don't shoot up into the air," I say.

"Also, they don't have the words 'deluxe' or 'supreme' on them," Dragon adds.

"How about we get him one of those slime kits?" Mom points to a display of different colored slime sets behind me.

A slime kit actually seems like it'd be a pretty good birthday gift.

"Okay," I agree. But I'm not finished with the volcano building set yet. "How much is the deluxe one?" I ask.

"About forty dollars after tax," my mom replies.

Dragon whistles. "That's more than a year's worth of claw manicures," he says.

I slump my shoulders in defeat. "I don't have forty dollars," I say.

"How much money do you have saved?" my mom asks.

I take a minute to add up my savings. There was the three dollars I got for my last tooth. But I had to give all three dollars to my twin sister, Ellie, when Dragon accidentally scorched her new shoelaces after he burped too close to her shoes. I also earned seven dollars for helping my dad rake the backyard. Until Dragon and I made a bet as to who could jump the highest into the pile, which splattered the leaves all over the yard. And then my dad made me give four dollars back.

"I have three dollars," I say.

"Does that include the dollar bill that someone left too close to my snout when I burped this morning?" Dragon asks.

I groan. "You have to stop burping," I tell him.

Dragon shrugs. "I can't. Burping is who I am."

I turn back to my mom. "I have two dollars," I tell her.

I think my mom is about to shake her head again, but she just sighs. "You could always earn your allowance by doing your chores."

"How much do I get for chores?" I ask.

"Two dollars a week," she replies.

I smack my hand against my forehead. Only two dollars a week? I'd need to do chores for . . . uh . . .

"That's nineteen weeks of chores to earn the thirty-eight dollars you need to buy the volcano building set," my mom says as though she can read my mind. "I'm going to pay for the slime kit now," she says, and takes it to one of the cashiers.

Dragon's eyes look like they're going to pop out of his head. "*NINETEEN WEEKS?*" he moans loudly. "I can't wait that long! I need to see gushing, red, molten, hot lava *now*."

"We need to find another way to get money besides just doing chores," I say.

"Hmmm...!" Dragon ponders. His eyes suddenly light up, and he runs over to the cashier where Mom is paying for the slime kit. "Excuse me, cashier person. You have a lot of money there. May I please have thirty-eight dollars? In return, I will bring you marshmallows tomorrow."

The cashier ignores Dragon as he hands Mom a receipt to sign.

Dragon huffs. "How about burnt marshmallows?"

The cashier still ignores Dragon.

Dragon pouts as he walks back to me.

"This money business is harder than it looks," he says, and then gives me a funny look. "Hey. You get money for your teeth from the tooth fairy, right?"

"Yeah," I say slowly. I have a feeling I won't like where this is going.

Dragon puts his snout right in my face as he opens my mouth with a claw. "You still have plenty of teeth in there, waiting to be traded for money! With a couple of good pulls, I can take them all out."

I push Dragon's claw away and shut my mouth tightly. I shake my head as hard as I can.

"Hmph," Dragon snorts, and stomps his feet.

"We can't just ask people to give us money," I tell Dragon. "We're going to have to earn it somehow. We need ideas."

Dragon stops stomping and looks at me with a smirk on his face.

"Oh, I can come up with ideas," he declares.

I cover my mouth with my hand in case he's thinking of pulling more teeth again.

"I can think of *lots* of ideas," Dragon adds.

That's what I'm afraid of.

2

The Super Easy Plan

After we get back home, Dragon and I have an emergency backyard meeting. I bring the marshmallows. He brings more marshmallows.

I begin the meeting by pacing back and forth over newly fallen leaves. "The meeting of how to make lots of money has begun," I declare.

Dragon doesn't reply because he's stuffed fourteen marshmallows into his mouth at once.

"We want a plan that's original yet super easy," I begin.

Dragon gulps down the marshmallows and points to a pile of dirt on the ground.

"You want to do something with dirt?" I ask.

Dragon shakes his head. "Of course not," he says. "First we'll add water to make it mud. And sell the mud."

I sigh. "No one is going to pay for mud. Everyone can just go into their own backyard, scoop up some dirt, and add water."

"Yeah, but ours will be toasty," Dragon counters, and blows a small huff of smoke onto the dirt.

I scrunch my nose at the smell.

"We need a new plan," I say.

"A plan for what?" a voice says. I know without looking that it's Ellie.

Ellie joins me and Dragon on the patio with her basketball and is bouncing it on the ground.

"A plan for ways to make money," I tell her.

Ellie shrugs and shoots the ball into the basketball hoop set up at the end of our driveway. Dragon tries to catch the ball as it falls back down by putting his arms in a circle, but it goes right through. Ellie picks up the ball and bounces it again.

"Just do your chores every week, save your allowance, and then you'll have money," she says.

"If I'd known that I'd need money *now*, I would have started doing my chores months ago," I say. I do not say I don't even remember what my chores are.

"I'm open!" Dragon shouts to Ellie with his arms extended. As usual, Ellie ignores him.

"What do you need money so much for?" Ellie asks, and throws me the ball.

I catch the ball before Dragon can get to it. I ignore Dragon and look at Ellie. "Uh, I need the money for something super important," I tell her. Ellie raises her eyebrows like she doesn't believe me.

"What? It *is* super important," I insist as I pass her the ball. Dragon tries to intercept but misses.

"You need to buy a hundred bags of marshmallows or something?" Ellie says, and rolls her
eyes. She turns away to shoot the ball again.

"Oh, that's not a bad idea!" Dragon says.

"*No,*" I practically shout. "I need the money
for ..."

"Charity," Dragon says.

"Charity," I say before I realize what I'm saying.

"*Charity?*" Ellie says, looking at me suspiciously. She's bouncing the ball again but misses it as she's momentarily distracted. Dragon lunges for the ball, dribbles it to the basket, shoots, and hits the rim.

"That was almost in!" Dragon yelps, and gleefully does a jig. I am very grateful no one else can see him move at this moment.

Ellie picks up the ball and shakes her head. "It must be windy today," she says. "Are you *really* doing something for charity, Warren?"

"Yes," I say. I do not say that the charity is obviously me and Dragon.

"Which one?" she asks, putting one hand on her hip and holding the ball with her other hand.

"Um . . . a toy one."

"Oh!" Ellie says. She smiles nicely at me for some reason. "Like how people collect toys to send to kids in the hospital?"

"Well . . ."

"I'm surprised," Ellie continues. "That's actually really generous. Especially for . . . you."

"Uh . . ." I'm not sure whether that was a compliment or not.

"My teacher was telling us about this very thing yesterday," Ellie says. "Last year for the holidays she helped her church raise money to buy a hundred new toys for kids in the hospital! I bet she'd be so happy to hear I'm going to raise the money to buy even more toys!" Ellie glances at me. "I mean . . . we'll raise the money."

"We don't really have to tell your teacher," I begin.

"Hi, Michael!" Ellie suddenly calls out. She waves to our next-door neighbor Michael. He's on his swing set. His older brother, Jayden, is standing nearby talking on his phone.

Michael's not my best friend, because Dragon is my best friend. But he's probably my best human friend. Even though Michael is in first grade and I'm in second, we get along really well.

Michael stops swinging and comes running. "Hey! My moms are baking with Addie," he says, referring to his younger sister.

"Warren is trying to earn money to buy toys for kids in the hospital," Ellie tells him.

Michael widens his eyes. "Wow! Really? My cousin Kaleb is going to the hospital this weekend to have his tonsils taken out. I bet a new toy would make him feel better."

"I'm *still* open!" Dragon says, and stomps his foot.

Michael turns to me and passes the ball. "How did you think up the idea?" he asks. "Did your parents tell you to? Do you know a kid in the hospital? I can't believe you're doing this, Warren."

"Why is everyone so surprised I'm doing something nice?" I say, forgetting for a moment that I'm not really doing something nice.

Dragon looks at me. "It's very nice of you to raise money for kids in the hospital," he says, and punches my shoulder.

I glare at Dragon.

He ignores me and continues. "Of course, we'll need to buy the volcano building set first, and then see how much money is left over for those sick kids. The only thing worse than a sick kid is a sick dragon. Because if I don't get the volcano building set, I'll be so upset I'll throw up. Or I'll wither away and die. Or both. I'll throw up as I wither away and die."

Dragon can be a little dramatic sometimes.

"Sorry," Michael says with a shrug. "It's really nice. Do you need help making money?"

"Yes," Dragon says. "We need lots of help. First, we need money. Second, we need ways to make more money. Third, we need marsh-mallows. Fourth, I need a nap because all this money talk is exhausting."

3

Ellie Makes a Decision

"I guess I can use help . . ." I say to Michael.

"Maybe Kaleb can come help us too!" Michael says.

"So, how should we raise money?" Ellie asks.

"A car wash?" Michael suggests. "All you need is soap, water, and lots of people to bring their cars."

"Besides our parents, and your brother Jayden, who do we know who drives?" Ellie asks.

Michael furrows his eyebrows. "That's a good point. Most of Jayden's friends don't even have cars to drive."

Dragon licks his lips and twiddles his claws.

"A bake sale?" I can already see he's imagining eating everything we bake before we can sell it. "Mmmm. Chocolate, marshmallows, chocolate marshmallows, mmmmmmm." There's no way he won't mess up a bake sale.

"Raking leaves?" Michael suggests. "I know my moms would pay us."

"I do need a good pile of leaves to jump into," Dragon ponders as he looks around the backyard. "Several piles, if I'm being honest."

"I don't think so," I say, remembering what happened the last time Dragon and I tried raking leaves to earn money.

"Then what?" Michael says.

"A bake sale!" Dragon practically screams. I shake my head and try to think about something Dragon won't mess up. Something he's good at that he'll actually be able to help us with. I don't think we could get anyone to pay for training worms to become ninja warriors, even though Dragon is really good at that.

And because of safety issues, fire breathing classes are probably out of the question. And dueling lessons. And building death-defying mazes.

I try to think about what I'd pay money for. Something fun. Something memorable. Something . . . magical. "Let's do a magic show!" I shout.

Michael and Ellie look at me with their mouths open. I'm guessing it's because I've never done a magic show before. But when you have a sidekick that no one else can see walking or talking, the possibilities are endless.

"Nobody's going to pay to see you pull your dragon doll out of a hat," Ellie scoffs.

"Did she just call me a doll?" Dragon says, and angrily puffs some smoke. He tries to take the ball from Ellie, but she passes it to Michael again too quickly.

"They will too pay for it," I protest. "We'll make stuff disappear! Saw people in half!"

"We can turn ten marshmallows into zero marshmallows," Dragon offers.

Ellie raises an eyebrow at me.

"That sounds pretty fun," Michael concedes as he dribbles in place. "I saw a magic show one day at camp and it was really cool. The magician made five balloons come out of a hat and I caught one! Can you do that trick? Can you do a trick with a basketball?"

Dragon grabs the ball as it bounces under Michael's hand and runs around the side of the house with it.

"I just made the basketball disappear," I say, and chuckle. Michael looks down.

"How'd you do that?" he asks with his mouth open.

Just then, Michael's mom Paula calls out to us. "The brownies are ready! Come join us, Ellie and Warren! They're nice and fresh."

Ellie smiles at Paula before whipping her head back toward me and Michael. "That's it!"

she exclaims. "We'll have a bake sale."

"Sheesh! That's what *I've* been saying," Dragon says, and throws his paws up in the air.

"I don't think a bake sale is a good idea," I tell Ellie.

Ellie puts her hands on her hips. "It's a perfect idea," she argues. "Everyone loves sweet stuff. And all we'll need, besides the food, is a bunch of tables."

"It does sound simple enough," Michael agrees.

"But this whole thing was all my idea," I sputter. "I was the one who thought of earning money in the first place. And I say we go with a magic show."

"Okay, let's put it to a vote," Ellie announces. "All in favor of earning money by organizing a bake sale, raise your hand." Ellie and Michael raise their hands. Dragon raises his paw.

"Two to one. It's settled. We're doing the bake sale," Ellie says happily. "We're going to

have the best bake sale fundraiser the town of Eddington has ever seen." Ellie suddenly looks into the distance with a weird smile on her face. "I'll probably get extra credit from my teacher. And Principal Fenly will talk about us during the morning announcements. Maybe we'll make it into the newspaper. And then someone will write a book about us and make it into a movie and ..."

"Hey! This is for the kids in the hospital,

remember?" I say, waving my hand in front of Ellie's face.

"I thought it was really about buying the volcano building set," Dragon says, pulling at my sleeve. I try to ignore him.

Ellie blinks a few times. She then looks at me sheepishly. "Of course. It's *definitely* all about the kids in the hospital. I was just thinking that a morning announcement and newspaper article could help advertise the bake sale."

"*And* the magic show," I say. Ellie raises her eyebrow at me but I'm not budging. I know I'll need a distraction for Dragon to keep him away from the bake sale. Plus, maybe if I make enough money from the magic show, people won't notice me taking some for my volcano building kit charity. I'll make money for that *and* the kids in the hospital. It'll be a win-win situation.

"How are we going to get in the newspaper?" Michael asks. "We're just kids."

"Brian Lee got in the paper when he had a lemonade stand to raise money for Eddington's food bank," Ellie says. "He said a lot of people came to the lemonade stand because they read about it. I bet Mom and Dad can help me call the paper and ask if they'll write about our bake sale."

"I've always wanted to be in the paper," Dragon says dreamily. "I hope I can get a manicure for my claws in time if they're going to take photos."

"We have to figure out when to actually have the bake sale," Ellie points out. "What about next Saturday?"

"That's soon!" Michael exclaims.

"Yeah, but it's starting to get colder," Ellie replies. "If we wait too long, no one will want to volunteer for something outdoors."

I realize that Michael, Ellie, and I are all wearing sweatshirts. Dragon doesn't need a sweatshirt because he's always warm.

"Next Saturday is good," I say. I'm pretty sure I don't have anything to do on the weekend until Avik's birthday party on Sunday.

Ellie scrunches her face up. "That'll only give us one week. And the paper comes out Wednesdays . . . But we can do this!" Ellie hits a fist into her other hand. "Michael," she says, pointing at him, "will you please ask Principal Fenly if we can use the school parking lot for the bake sale?"

"And for the magic show," I add.

Ellie harrumphs.

"Sure," Michael replies.

"Great. I'll contact the paper," Ellie announces. "Then we should tell our parents and ask them if they'll help us with baking. And, Michael, you and I should call kids from school to see if they'll bring treats. I'll also make posters to put up around town."

"I'll taste test after the baked goods are made," Dragon offers.

Ellie looks at me warily. "What are you going to do?"

"I'm gonna make some magic," I say.

4

Distractions

It turns out that making magic is hard when there are distractions. Dragon and I are supposed to be practicing how to escape from being tied up inside a locked cardboard box, when we hear my dad return from the supermarket with Ellie.

"We got all the ingredients to make the s'mores cookies for the bake sale!" we hear Ellie whoop as they enter the house.

Dragon's ears perk up, and before I know it, he's escaped not only the locked cardboard box, but our practice session as well.

I push the knotted bedsheets and rope to

the side of my room and head downstairs to the kitchen. Dragon is peering into the grocery bags next to my mom.

"You guys got enough flour, eggs, chocolate chips, and mini marsh-mallows to make hundreds of cookies!" Mom says, nodding her head as though she's impressed. "We can bake and freeze some now and then make the rest the day before the bake sale."

"I don't think it's going to be enough," Dragon says, and scrunches his face up like he's worried. He starts to count on his claws. "After I taste test a few hundred cookies, how many will be left over for the actual bake sale?"

"This is great!" Ellie says. "Michael said his moms will make a ton of brownies. Now I just have to call friends from school to see if anyone can come and help."

Ellie brings out our school directory and starts to scan the list of names.

"Do you think Alison Cohen will want to help?" she asks me. Alison is a girl in my class at school.

"Probably," I say, thinking that Alison is pretty nice. "I'll call her," I say, and reach for the phone. I've called Alison before and it only ended with her hanging up on me twice, so I think it went pretty well.

"Hello?" Alison answers.

"Hi, Alison," I say. "It's Warren. We're going to have a bake sale and a magic show next Saturday at one o'clock in the school parking lot to raise money to buy toys for kids in the hospital." I glance at Ellie. She nods her head like I'm doing okay so far. "It was my idea."

"Wow!" Alison exclaims. "Raising money to get toys for kids in the hospital is really nice. *You* thought of it?"

"YES!" I shout. I did not mean to shout.

"Why is everyone surprised I thought of it?"

"You didn't think of it," Dragon says.

"Um, no reason," Alison replies.

"If you want to help, you can either bring food for the bake sale, or . . . " I pause for dramatic effect. ". . . get sawed in half at the magic show."

Ellie and my mom slap their hands against their foreheads at the same time.

I hear Alison sigh over the phone.

"So will you come?" I ask.

"I can bring cupcakes for the bake sale," Alison says.

"*And* get sawed in half?"

I hear a click.

"Well?" Ellie says.

"She only hung up on me once," I say. "I think I'm getting better at phone calls."

Ellie won't let me call anyone else.

"Who am I going to saw in half?" I say out loud. My mom looks away as she fits the egg cartons into the fridge. Ellie pretends she doesn't hear me while she dials another student.

Dragon looks up from counting the bags of chocolate chips. "I'm too muscular to saw in half," he says, and flexes his arms. I don't notice any muscles.

Out of the corner of my eye, I see my dad walking by in the hallway.

"Dad!" I shout as I run over to him. He stops walking and glances down at me. "Can I practice sawing you in half for the magic show?"

"Uh," he stammers, "I have to help with the baking." Dad rushes to the kitchen.

If no one helps me practice, I won't have a good enough show to earn money for the toy charity *and* the volcano building kit. I need help. I need a miracle.

I hear someone knock at our front door.

"My hands are covered in cookie dough," I hear my mom shout. "Warren, you need to answer the door."

"I need a lot of things," I grumble as I open the door. Surprisingly, I just might get one of them.

5

Kaleb to the Rescue

Michael is standing outside with a boy who looks a little older than us. He's taller than me and doesn't wear glasses like Michael does.

"Warren, this is my cousin Kaleb," Michael says.

"Hi," I say to Kaleb, and motion for both of them to come in.

"Hey!" Kaleb replies with a big grin.

"Kaleb will be in the hospital for his tonsils when we have the charity event this weekend," Michael says. "But he said he wanted to help out beforehand."

A clanging sound comes from the kitchen.

Michael, Kaleb, and I pause to listen.

"Bill!" my mom shouts. "Be careful!"

"That wasn't my fault!" Dad yells.

"It wasn't me," I hear Ellie say.

I see Dragon scurry through the kitchen doorway carrying mini chocolate chips in his paws.

"It wasn't *my* fault," he quickly tells me before he heads down the hall.

Suddenly there's a crashing sound from the kitchen.

"Okay, *that* was my fault," I hear my dad say.

"We can definitely use help around here," I tell Kaleb. "There's going to be a bake sale and a magic show."

"I'll help with the magic show!" Kaleb says suddenly. "I love magic," he explains. "And I'm not so great with baking."

Michael snorts. "Like that time you burned the toast because you—" Kaleb stops him by waving his hands in front of Michael's face. I laugh because Kaleb and Michael remind me of myself and Ellie. "Okay." Michael relents. "I'm going to find Ellie."

"She's in the kitchen," I tell Michael. "Come on, Kaleb," I say, and he follows me to my room.

Kaleb walks over to the cardboard box and picks it up. "Is this for the magic show?" he asks.

"For the disappearing act," I tell him.

"That sounds complicated," Kaleb says, and rubs his chin. "You probably want to do something simple but fun."

"I'm also planning to saw someone in half," I say.

Kaleb laughs. "That's funny," he says like I made a joke. I laugh back although I'm not sure what joke I just made.

"I'll tell you what's funny!" Dragon says as he barges in through the door. There are no more mini chocolate chips in his paws, but there are smudges of chocolate around his snout. "It's funny to think that six measly bags of chocolate chips are enough for the bake sale."

I look away from Dragon when Kaleb pulls

out a pack of cards from his back pocket. "I brought these when Michael said you're working on a magic show," Kaleb explains.

He spreads out the cards on my carpet and sits down. I see that the cards are all turned on the patterns side so you can't see what cards they are underneath.

"Pick a card, any card," Kaleb says dramatically as he waves his hands over the cards.

"Oooh! That one!" Dragon says and hops up and down a little when he points to a card. "And that one too! Also, that one."

"I'm just supposed to pick one, right?" I ask, looking at Dragon pointedly.

"Yep, just one," Kaleb replies. "But don't tell me which card you pick. Just look at it quickly so you remember it, and then put it at the top, right here."

Dragon leans over my shoulder to see as I pick out a red queen of hearts and place it pattern side up at the top of the pile. Kaleb pushes the cards together and shuffles them a few times.

"When's the magic going to happen?" Dragon whispers to me. "Are the cards going to burst into flames? Does he turn the cards into lava that shoots up into the air?"

Kaleb stops shuffling and pulls out a card from the pile. He places it in front of me and turns it over. It's the queen of hearts.

I'm impressed, but I see Dragon roll his eyes.

"That's it?" Dragon says. "You didn't even saw the card in half. Warren, no one's going to pay a lot of money to see a little card trick."

I'm worried Dragon has a point. I need to raise enough money to give some to the charity *and* pay for the volcano building set. What if card tricks aren't interesting enough?

"How'd you do the trick?" I ask Kaleb.

"Magic." Kaleb smiles and wiggles his eyebrows. "I can show you how I did it and a few more tricks. I love magic." He suddenly frowns. "I wish I could do them at your magic show with you, but I'll be in the hospital."

"I'm sorry," I say. I realize I wish Kaleb could go to the charity event too. I feel bad he has to go to the hospital at all, and I start to wonder what it would be like if I had to go.

Surgery might hurt. I wonder if Dragon would be able to stay with me during the surgery. I wonder if anyone would bring me marshmallows and cookies after the surgery. I wonder if you can't eat marshmallows or cookies after surgery.

Kaleb shrugs. "It's okay. Let me show you another trick."

I spend the next couple of hours learning card tricks from Kaleb and practicing them. Dragon alternates between hanging out with us and traveling down to the kitchen. Whenever he returns, he has a new glob of chocolate somewhere on his face.

I'm practicing a new trick Kaleb's taught me when Dragon comes barreling into the bedroom with chocolate smeared over his forehead.

"Do some magic and hide me!" he cries out, furiously looking around for a place to hide. He ends up diving under the bedcovers.

Ellie and Michael run into my room soon after.

"Have you been in here this whole time?" Ellie asks us suspiciously.

"Yeah," I say, and Kaleb nods. "Why?"

"Half of the chocolate chips went missing," Michael explains.

"I told you they didn't buy enough," I hear Dragon whisper.

"It wasn't us," Kaleb tells them.

"Well, we have to go downstairs now anyway," Michael adds.

"What's going on?" I ask.

Ellie smiles triumphantly. "We're going to be famous," she says.

6

Famous

Dragon peeks his head out from the bedcovers. "We're going to be famous?" he says. "I've always wanted to be famous. Or infamous."

"A reporter from the newspaper came to interview us about the bake sale," Ellie says.

"*And* the magic show," I add.

"And the magic show," Ellie concedes with an eye roll. She peers into a small mirror on my dresser to redo her ponytail. Ellie doesn't notice as Dragon checks himself in the mirror behind her. He notices the chocolate smear and furiously tries to wipe it off.

"Do I look okay?" Dragon asks me. "I would

have gotten my weekly facial if I'd known I'd become famous today."

Dragon looks . . . like Dragon. I nod my head yes and Dragon smiles.

We head down the stairs where my parents are talking with a man I guess is the news-paper reporter. He's carrying a medium-size black bag.

My mom sees us and makes the introduc-tions to the reporter, Mr. Harris. "Why don't you kids and Mr. Harris have the interview in the living room?" she suggests, and leads the way. Mom, Kaleb, and Mr. Harris take a seat on the couch. Michael sits on the bean bag, and my dad brings in chairs from the kitchen for me, Ellie, and himself to sit on.

From the black bag, Mr. Harris takes out a pen and a notepad. I'm expecting a tape recorder or something else, but he just starts jotting down some notes before talking.

"So," he begins, "how did you guys think up the idea of raising money in the first place?"

To my surprise, everyone except for Mr. Harris looks straight at me.

I clear my throat. I hadn't expected to be the first one to talk to the reporter. "Well, first I thought of toys," I tell Mr. Harris.

"One toy," Dragon corrects me. "One very special lava-ish toy."

I try not to roll my eyes at Dragon before I continue. "And then I thought of a charity."

"I actually thought of the charity idea,"

Dragon interrupts. "That's because, for some weird reason, no one pays dragons money for sitting around all day looking cute." I can't help myself. I have to roll my eyes.

"And Ellie thought of a bake sale," I say. Ellie smiles at me. "But I thought of the magic show." Ellie stops smiling. She looks more worried than annoyed though, but turns to Mr. Harris to speak.

"Michael and Kaleb have been helping us with both," she says.

Dragon walks over to Mr. Harris on the couch and hops on the seat next to him. "Excuse me, but Warren rudely forgot to introduce me," he huffs, glaring at me. "My name is Dragon. I'm known for my cunning, my bravery, and my sportsmanlike conduct. Also, I've never once brushed my teeth, yet I've never had a cavity. Honestly, we'd need all day to go over all of my attributes. Hey, you're not writing this down." Dragon looks at me. "Why isn't he writing any of this down?"

I try to duck my head.

Mr. Harris asks us a bunch more questions. Then he takes some photos of me, Ellie, Michael, and Kaleb. Dragon sneaks into most of the photos.

Soon after Mr. Harris leaves, it's time for Michael and Kaleb to go, too. I thank Kaleb for helping me with the card tricks. He says I can keep the pack of cards he brought over and wishes me luck.

I figure I should go practice what Kaleb taught me before I forget it, when Ellie stops me.

"You're really set on having a magic show at our bake sale?" she says with her arms crossed.

"Yes," I reply.

"Fine. But you'd better have a good one ready. Especially if we get a big crowd from people seeing the newspaper article."

"It's going to be a *great* magic show," I declare.

"Do you even know what magic tricks you're going to do?" Ellie asks suspiciously.

"Yes," I answer. I do not say I'm not totally sure what magic tricks I'm going to do.

"You're not really going to just do some card tricks like I saw you practicing in your room with Kaleb, right?"

"Wha . . . what?" I sputter. "I'm going to do something way more awesome than some card tricks."

Ellie looks relieved. "Good," she says.

Abandoning my plans to practice the card tricks, I try to find Dragon. I'm going to need his help. Unfortunately, I find him sleeping underneath the kitchen table. A full day of stealing chocolate chips and getting famous can really wear out a dragon.

7

Magic Trick

All week I see everyone get ready for the bake sale. Ellie, my parents, Michael, and Michael's family are busy working on it before and after school. Businesses around town let Ellie put her posters up in their windows. At school, Principal Fenly has Michael read an announcement about the charity event over the loudspeaker after the morning school news. My parents fill part of our hallway with supplies to bring on Saturday.

So what am I doing to prepare? More specifically, what are Dragon and I doing to prepare?

Well, we were going to practice our disappearing Dragon act. But when Dragon hid, he fell asleep and forgot to come back. Then I tried to pull Dragon out of a hat, but he got stuck and I had to cut the hat carefully to let him out. It wasn't easy because Dragon kept squirming, worried I'd accidentally nick one of his wings, but he was fine.

By Wednesday, I'm started to get a little worried. And by *a little*, I mean I'm starting to panic. If I don't have a good magic show, I won't make any extra money to buy me and Dragon the volcano building kit.

Ellie doesn't help my panic when she finds the town newspaper in our mailbox. We walk home from school with our dad and she rushes ahead to check the mail.

"It's here!" she shouts, holding up the paper.

"Let's take a look," Dad says happily as he opens our front door.

Dragon bounces down the stairs to join us.

"What'd you bring me?" he asks me. Dragon always expects me to bring him something on my way home from school.

"I can't wait to find the article about us in the paper," Ellie says, and marches into the kitchen with our dad right behind her.

"Oh, you brought the paper!" Dragon clasps his claws together. "Can we get copies to hand out to everyone who doesn't know me? Because I feel like having my photo in the paper will help people understand how important I am."

"I don't have any money to buy more papers," I tell Dragon. "That's the whole point of the magic show, remember?"

"Oh, yeah," Dragon says. He looks disappointed.

"Come on," I say. "Let's go see if they wrote about us."

Dragon follows me into the kitchen. Ellie has opened up the paper on the kitchen table. The front page has something to do with the upcoming mayoral elections. The next page is filled with scores from the high school sports teams.

"Where's the bake sale info?" Ellie huffs as she flips the pages.

"I can't believe we aren't front page news," Dragon says.

Ellie turns another page and lets out a squeal. "Here we are!" She points to a photo Mr. Harris took of Ellie, Michael, me, and Kaleb. Ellie, Michael, and Kaleb are all smiling in the photo. Dragon is also there in the photo, smiling as he positions himself in between Kaleb and Michael. I'm not smiling in the photo, because I'm looking at Dragon with a worried expression on my face.

"You don't look so happy in the photo, Warren," Dragon points out. "Didn't you hear when Mr. Harris told us to smile? I look very happy because I remembered to smile. See how shiny my pearly whites are?"

I slap my hand against my forehead.

"Why is your dragon in the photo?" Ellie asks

me, but then shrugs. I can see she's starting to read the article below the photo.

The article discusses how we came up with the idea for the bake sale and gives details about the Saturday event, suggesting that people stop by to help us raise money. At the end of the article, it mentions there will also be a magic show.

"This is a great article on your event, kids," Dad says. "You should be proud of yourselves."

"Thanks, Dad," Ellie says, beaming.

Dad turns to me. "Warren, how's everything going with your magic show? Are you all prepared?"

"Well, I just need to make a few adjustments," I tell Dad. "And practice." I nudge Dragon toward the kitchen door. "I should probably do that now, actually."

"Okay. Just make sure you get your homework done first," Dad calls out to me after we leave the room.

"We have to figure out something for the magic show," I tell Dragon as we walk up the stairs to my bedroom.

"I can't work on an empty stomach!" Dragon moans, and flops down on my bed.

"Why don't you just get a snack from the kitchen?" I suggest.

Dragon frowns. "I ate them already."

I sigh. "What about all the cookies in the freezer? Take a couple out and after a little while they'll defrost. Just don't take too many since they're for the bake sale."

Dragon looks up at the ceiling and starts to twiddle his claws. That's never a good sign.

"What did you do?" I ask.

"Oh, nothing," Dragon replies. "I, um, don't want to take any cookies away from the bake sale. That wouldn't be right."

"You didn't eat them all already, did you?" I ask. I'm starting to get nervous.

"No, no," Dragon insists. "The cookies are definitely still in the freezer."

I'm still suspicious but I can't figure out what Dragon did.

"Don't worry," Dragon says suddenly, hopping off the bed. "You do your homework, and I'll find something to eat."

I shrug and start my math sheet. All of a sudden, my pillow comes flying over, landing on my head.

"Hey!" I say, pushing the pillow onto the floor.

"Found a cookie on your bed!" Dragon announces, holding one up.

"Great!" I mutter, returning to my homework. A moment later, I feel a bump on my chair. I look down to see one of my sneakers lying next to the chair leg.

"Found two marshmallows in your closet!" Dragon says, and stuffs them into his mouth.

I watch as Dragon moves through my room, throwing items about and finding snacks. I don't want to clean everything up, but I have to admit it looks pretty funny.

And then I realize, I actually have an idea for the magic show. A great idea.

8

Cotton Cookies

Saturday finally arrives, and everyone besides me and Dragon is freaking out. We're supposed to drive over to the school to get ready for the bake sale in just a few minutes.

"Where are the signs to put in front of the bake sale tables?" Ellie yells as she runs past me and Dragon in the downstairs hallway.

"In the den where you put glitter all over them!" Mom shouts back.

"Are you ready, Warren?" Dad asks me as he carries trays to the car. "I've already packed your sign for the magic show in the trunk. Do you need to bring anything else out to the car?"

"Nope," I say. "I'm all prepared." I pat my back pocket where I've kept Kaleb's pack of cards. I'm not planning to use them, but I feel I should bring them anyway like a good-luck charm.

Dad raises an eyebrow as he looks at me, obviously surprised. "Okay," he says. "Help me bring more supplies out, okay?" I grab a bag full of napkins and we load everything into the trunk.

Ellie comes out with her signs and some clipboards. "Where's your stuff for the magic show?" she asks me.

"I don't need to bring anything," I tell her.

"What about a hat and rabbit?" Ellie says, looking anxious. "A saw? A wand?"

I shake my head. "A true magician doesn't need any props." Dragon coughs loudly. "Well, other than Dragon," I say. Dragon smiles.

"I think we've got everything!" Mom exclaims as she shoves a few clipboards into the already packed trunk.

We get into the car and head toward the

school parking lot. Usually we just walk to school since it's only a couple of blocks from our house, but we're bringing so much stuff for the bake sale today that we need the car.

When we arrive, Principal Fenly, Michael and his family, and a few people who agreed to volunteer are already there. I see Alison walking over with her parents. They're carrying a few large plastic containers that I bet contain cupcakes.

Ellie quickly gets out of our car with a clipboard and starts talking with people about where to set up. Soon more people show up and bring more treats with them to sell.

With everyone else working to set up the bake sale, Dragon and I are left alone to put up the magic show sign. I bring over a small table to stand on before Dragon and I each take a side of the sign and tape it to the side of the building.

I know that it will be a few minutes before actual customers are supposed to arrive, so I wander over to the bake sale tables. I spot the s'mores cookies that Ellie made with our parents, the brownies that Michael's family brought, and Alison's cupcakes. There are also doughnuts, sprinkle cookies, fudge bars, and chocolate covered pretzels.

Principal Fenly tells Ellie and Michael they've done a great job setting up. Ellie beams and Michael gives a small smile.

I hear my stomach grumble and wish I had eaten more than three bowls of cereal at breakfast.

I'm about to sneak a cookie when I hear Ellie squeal. "It's starting!" she shouts, and proudly smiles at a family lined up to be the first customers.

I retract my hand from the cookie platter and check the magic show area. No one's walking over there yet. My stomach is grumbling even louder now, and I figure I have a couple of minutes to get a treat before starting the show.

I wait to see that Ellie's busy with a new customer before reaching over for a brownie.

"Warren, those are one dollar each," Michael's mom Nia tells me.

"Even for performers?" I ask.

Nia smiles at me. "All right, just this once," she says, and goes to pick up a brownie. "Huh. That's odd."

"What's odd?" I ask.

Nia points to the brownies, counting them. "I thought we brought more than this," she says. "Well, we'll sell what we have." Nia still looks confused as she hands me a brownie on a napkin.

I thank her and start to eat the brownie when I hear someone shout, "YUCK!" I accidentally drop the brownie on the ground and groan. The kid that yelled is now spitting a cookie into his napkin. "That's gross," he proclaims, and points to the cookies on the table.

"What's wrong?" Ellie asks, her face scrunched up in confusion.

"There's something weird in those s'mores cookies," he says. "I want my money back."

My dad picks up a s'mores cookie and starts to break it apart. "What in the world . . ." he says, squinting at the cookie pieces. "These aren't marshmallows. These are pieces of cotton balls!"

"Disgusting!" Ellie moans. "How did that happen?"

Everyone looks around, trying to figure out how mini marshmallows got replaced by pieces of cotton balls.

I have a feeling I know exactly how this happened. I look around the blacktop for Dragon. He's usually pretty easy to spot, but there are a lot of people and I don't see him right away.

"Warren," my mom calls out, and waves me over. "Maybe you should start the magic show while we figure this out."

I nod my head, but I can feel myself start to panic. I can't do the magic show without Dragon. I quickly look around the bake sale area but can't see Dragon under the tables or anywhere else.

"Ladies and gentlemen," Ellie's voice says over a bullhorn. "We're going to take a short break from the bake sale to figure out this, uh, situation. In the meantime, please enjoy my brother Warren's magic show!"

I gulp as I watch the customers slowly make their way over.

9

Real Magic

Luckily, when I look back at the magic show area, Dragon is already there under the sign.

I rush over to him. "We're going to talk about the cotton ball thing you did to the cookies later," I tell him. "But right now, we have to put on the magic show."

Dragon covers his mouth with his hand and yawns. "It's not my fault they didn't buy enough mini marshmallows," he says with a shrug. "It took a lot of time to switch the cotton balls for the marshmallows. I work hard for my sustenance."

Dragon crosses his arms, and that's when I

notice his mouth. "Seriously?" I say.

"What now?" Dragon asks.

I smack my hand onto my forehead. "You had to steal brownies too?"

Dragon licks his lips where there are brownie globs stuck on. "I knew there was some left over." He smiles and wipes his mouth clean with his tongue. Dragon pats his belly and gives another yawn.

"Stop yawning. It's time for the show," I tell him before turning around to face the crowd that's assembled. "Welcome to the best ever magic show!" Then I bow. I'm not sure why I bow, but I feel like it's something a magician would do. Dragon takes his cue from me and also bows.

"What kind of magic show is this?" says Nicky, a boy from my class. I recognize Nicky and a few other faces of kids from school, but some of the people I don't know.

"I told you, it's the best magic show ever," I

MAgic Show today!!!
real magic
no joke! that's right

say. "It only costs one dollar to be completely amazed! Behold the wonders of my magical mind. I can see things no one can see. I can hear things no one can hear. I can ... do magical stuff. Take an object, any object, and hold it in your hand."

Everyone watching reaches into their pocket or bags to pull out something. I see Nicky take out a small green bouncing ball.

"Now, I am going to turn around. When I do, hide your object somewhere. On the count of three, I will turn back around and know exactly where you've hidden it."

I hear Nicky snort in disbelief as I turn around. A lot of other people there don't look too convinced that I know what I'm doing. I smile as I begin to count. "One . . . two . . . three."

I turn around to see that everyone has put their object somewhere. I nod at Dragon. We walk from person to person. Dragon points to where they hid their object, and I call out the hiding place.

"Under your shoe!" I tell a man who has put a business card under his shoe. He reaches down to get it and looks surprised. Some people nearby gasp.

"That's right!" the man says, impressed.

Dragon then points to Nicky's baseball cap before letting out another yawn. "Under your cap!" I tell Nicky. His eyes open wide as he takes off his cap to reveal the green ball.

"How'd you do that?" he asks.

I roll my eyes. "Magic," I say like it's obvious.

Alison is the last person I get to. Based on Dragon's motions to her pocket, I point to it, and Alison pulls out a barrette. She looks as stunned as everyone else.

They all start to clap and I bow again. I smile at Dragon. We make a good team sometimes.

"For the next magic trick, please hold out one dollar, which I will make disappear." I collect all the dollar bills and put them into my back pocket.

Everything is going according to plan. I just had the easiest, most successful magic show ever.

I look over to give Dragon a thumbs-up sign, but he's no longer standing next to me. In fact, he's no longer standing at all. Dragon is at my feet, curled up like he's about to fall asleep. I lean down and nudge his shoulder.

"Dragon, wake up," I whisper.

"Mmmm . . . food coma . . ." he moans. I can tell he's fallen fast asleep when he starts to snore.

"Is that the whole show?" Nicky asks. I stand up and count the money. It's only twenty-one dollars. Not nearly enough for the volcano building kit, let alone enough to give money to the charity too.

I check my back pocket and pull out the pack of cards Kaleb's gave me. I might as well try it. "I've got a few tricks left," I tell Nicky before walking to the small table I had stepped on earlier to hang the sign.

After taking a deep breath, I wave the cards in the air and try to mimic Kaleb's dramatic tone. "Ready for some real magic?" I ask the crowd. They shout back, "Ready!"

I spread the cards on the table and ask for a volunteer. Alison raises her hand right away and I point at her. She comes forward to the table and everyone else gathers around.

I feel my palms get a little sweaty, wishing I had practiced the card tricks more during the week. "Okay," I say. "Pick a card. Any card."

The first trick actually goes okay and I find the card Alison had picked easily. But my palms are still sweaty, and I mess up with the second volunteer. Nicky snorts again, but no one else seems too upset, so I try a few different tricks. Mostly I remember what to do, and silently thank Kaleb for all the time he spent teaching me.

After each successful card trick, I hold out a hat to collect dollar bills. Sometimes the people

watching are extra generous and put in more than a dollar. Eventually I notice that the crowd has thinned as people either return to the bake sale or leave the school lot.

"Good magic show," Alison says before walking away.

"Thanks!" I call back, and see it's a good time to pack up. As I put the cards back in the pack, I see Dragon start to stir.

"That was a good nap," he says, and stretches his arms. "Are we rich yet?" he asks, pointing to the money in the hat. I count the money.

"We have enough money for the volcano building kit *and* for the charity," I tell Dragon.

"Yay!" Dragon whoops and claps. "We should celebrate by eating whatever is left at the bake sale."

I'm about to follow him when Principal Fenly walks up.

"I heard you had an impressive magic show today, Warren," she says.

"Yeah, thanks," I say.

"How much money did you raise?"

"Uh, how much money?"

Principal Fenly points to the money in my hand. "How much money did you make from your magic show? I'm sure the children who receive toys will be very appreciative."

I look down at the money. "I'm not sure. I think it's seventy-three dollars?"

"That's wonderful!" Principal Fenly says with a smile. She suddenly turns to Ellie and my parents, who are gathered at a table counting the money from the bake sale proceeds. "Warren raised seventy-three dollars!" Everyone turns to look at me. Ellie looks surprised. Mom and Dad look proud. Dragon looks happy, as he's about to stuff four brownies into his mouth. He doesn't realize what's going on. I need a plan to keep the money.

Then everyone starts to clap and I hear Michael call out, "Yay, Warren!"

It's too late for a plan.

"I hope you feel very proud of yourself," Principal Fenly says, and pats me on the shoulder. She reaches for the dollar bills in my hand, and just like that, they disappear.

10

Two Toys

The next day, everyone is still happy with me. Like, really happy. Too happy.

"I'm sorry I ever doubted your magic show," Ellie says at breakfast. It's the third time she's apologized to me. It's getting weird. "Your magic show even made up for the lost money from those awful cotton cookies!"

"He did great," Mom says with a big grin. "Who knew you were such a professional magician, Warren!"

"Well, we already knew he could disappear when it's time to clean his room," Dad says, and everyone laughs. Everyone but me and Dragon.

"Seriously, Warren, you did a great job. Seventy-three dollars will buy some nice toys for kids in the hospital."

Dragon snorts. "I bet those kids are going to get a volcano building kit," he says angrily, tapping a spoon against the kitchen table. He's the only one who's not happy with me. "All because of *my* hard work," he adds. "Well, the hard work I put in before my nap."

I stir my cereal slowly. I'm not really hungry. Dragon's mad at me for losing the money. And even though I'd normally be happy that my family is impressed by me, it doesn't feel right. They all thought I was actually trying to help raise money for kids in the hospital, and I wasn't. I wish I could feel good about their praise, but I can't.

"Can I please be excused?" I say.

"You're not hungry?" Mom says, looking at my half-finished bowl. I shake my head. "All right, but we leave in an hour for Avik's party."

❈ ❈ ❈

An hour later, Mom pulls into the parking lot in front of Tony's Tops Toy Store.

"What are we doing here?" I ask.

"Avik's party is here," Mom explains. "They have a party room in the back."

Dragon is looking out the car window at the store. "Think anyone will notice if you take home the volcano building kit as a party favor?" he asks.

I shake my head and sigh. Dragon looks sad. "Maybe I can bring back some cake," I tell him. He looks a little happier.

I take the birthday gift for Avik, wave bye to Mom and Dragon, and head into the store. Avik and his parents greet me and other kids arriving and have us walk to the back room.

"Remember to put your name on a slip of paper and put it in the bowl for the toy giveaway!" Avik calls out as I make my way to the room.

A bunch of the kids at the party were also at the charity event. I get a lot of congratulations on the magic show and for raising so much money. I try to shrug like it's no big deal, because it shouldn't be. For me, at least. Ellie and Michael and everyone else should get the praise.

The party is pretty fun. We build our own robots and make our own puzzles before pizza and cake come out. It's ice cream cake so I don't try to save a piece for Dragon.

Before it's time to go, Avik's dad announces that it's time to pick the winner of the toy lottery. Avik reaches his hand into the bowl.

"The winner is . . . Warren!"

I drop the spoon I'm holding with cake on it. "Me?" I ask in disbelief.

"You have a choice, Warren," Avik's dad tells me. He points to two brand-new toys on a counter, still in their boxes. My mouth drops open. One of the toys is the Deluxe Volcano Building Set Supreme! The other toy is a box

filled with magic tricks. I can't believe it. I finally can have the volcano building set! Dragon will be so happy. We can shoot lava into the air to our heart's content.

"You deserve it, Warren!" Alison suddenly says from across the table. "You raised money to give toys to other kids, and now you get one of your own!"

Everyone nods their heads like they're agreeing with her. I look around the room. They really think I did a good thing for the right reasons. But it was really Kaleb who deserves the praise. It's because of his card tricks I made most of the money in the first place.

I think for a moment. I'm feeling a new feeling I haven't really felt before. Maybe ... I want to do a good thing. And maybe for the first time, I have the right reason for doing it.

I point to the toy that I've chosen.

Lava Magic

"NOOOOOOO!" I hear a wail from behind me. Dragon is trying to hide behind the table of presents. He must have followed me into the party room.

I walk over to the table and crouch down. "What are you doing here?" I whisper.

Dragon shows me three empty cake plates. "I was worried you weren't going to bring me back a big enough slice of cake," he says.

I can't blame him for that.

"Why didn't you pick the volcano building kit?" he asks. "We finally had a chance to see lava shoot up in the air. And we can do magic on our own. We don't even need a box of magic tricks."

"I'm sorry," I say. "But I know someone who deserves it."

❈ ❈ ❈

Mom picks us up from the party and we get into her car.

"I won a toy in a raffle at the party," I tell her, holding up the magic tricks box.

"That's great, Warren!" she says, and then turns to start the car.

"Mom, before you drive, can you call one of Michael's moms?" Mom switches the car off and turns around to look at me. "I have another toy to bring to a kid in the hospital," I say.

❈ ❈ ❈

A couple of hours later we're talking with Kaleb's parents outside of Kaleb's hospital room. They seem happy to see us, and tell me Kaleb just woke up from a nap so I can go in to say hi for a few minutes.

Dragon follows along as I walk in the room.

Kaleb is lying on a hospital bed. He looks happy to see me but tired. "Hi," Kaleb says with a small smile on his face.

"Hi," I say, and give a wave. I go sit down on a chair by the bed. Dragon walks over to a table that's piled with balloons and gift bags. He looks inside them all.

"These gummy bears are okay, but no marshmallows," Dragon says. "Sheesh. Don't people know the proper way to make a kid feel better?"

"I brought you this," I tell Kaleb, and hand over the magic tricks box.

Kaleb's eyes widen. "Wow!" he says, and takes it in his hands. "This is really cool! Thanks, Warren!"

For the first time since before the magic show, it feels good to be thanked.

"I wish I had a toy I could give you," Kaleb says.

"Oh, that's okay," I tell him. "I wanted to give
you this to say thanks for showing me the card
tricks. They were a big hit at the charity event!
And I have some ideas about how to earn money
for what I really want. A Deluxe Volcano Building Set Supreme. I want to see lava shoot up into
the air."

"That sounds fun," Kaleb says, and then
laughs. "It'd be like seeing flaming mud or
something."

Dragon stops rummaging through the bags and turns to Kaleb. "What did he say?" Dragon points to Kaleb. "Did he just say lava is like . . . flaming mud?" I can see that Dragon is starting to think of an idea. Dragon thinking of an idea always makes me nervous. "We have mud in the backyard," Dragon continues. "And I, well, I can provide the flame." Dragon suddenly sprouts a mischievous grin on his face.

I shake my head at Dragon but he doesn't notice.

"Kaleb, I hope you feel better soon," Dragon says quickly, taking a handful of gummy bears in his paw. "But I must run home now to perfect my own dragon-made lava kit."

I grab on to Dragon but he tries to wiggle away. We fall down to the floor.

"Are you . . . wrestling your dragon doll?" Kaleb asks, leaning over to see us.

"No!" I shout, and pull Dragon up with me. "I just, uh, slipped there."

Dragon tries to pull away again. "Listen," I

say, blocking the exit with my body. "Your dad said I could only stay a few minutes, but maybe we could meet up when you go back home to work on the magic tricks together?"

"I'd like that!" Kaleb says.

"Great!" I say.

Suddenly, Dragon pulls out of my grasp and runs out the door.

I rush out after him and see my mom talking with Kaleb's parents.

"Mom! We have to get home!"

"What's wrong?" she asks.

"Oh, nothing. I just forgot to do something," I say. I do not say I need to stop Dragon from accidentally lighting our backyard on fire. Dragon doesn't have a car to get home in, but he's surprisingly fast with those wings.

She says a quick goodbye before taking me home.

As soon as the car is parked, I unbuckle my seat belt and rush out toward the back. I don't see any smoke or fire.

Instead, I see Dad, Ellie, and Michael on the patio, putting something together. Dragon got back before me because he's also there, looking at a box.

"What's going on?" I ask.

Ellie looks up and smiles. "I got you something," she says. "Well, I got it for both of us. And I invited Michael over to play. But it's my way of saying sorry for being mean about your magic show. You really came through for the charity."

"We finally can shoot lava up in the air!" Dragon squeals, and I look more closely at the box he's holding. It's the Deluxe Volcano Building Set Supreme.

"You got this?" I ask Ellie.

"I had some allowance saved," Ellie says, and shrugs slightly. "Dad took me to the toy store this morning after Mom mentioned you wanted the volcano building set. You were at the birthday party in the back so you didn't see us. I thought it'd be a good surprise."

"Wow, thanks!" I say, and start looking at

the parts we're supposed to put together. "You didn't have to," I add.

"I think it will be fun," Ellie says. "Watching lava shoot up in the air is kinda like . . ."

"Magic," I say.

Dragon jumps up and down. "Lava magic," he says. "There's nothing better."

Join Warren & Dragon on a new adventure in: Warren & Dragon: Scary Sleepover, coming soon!

"Hi, Michael," Dragon and I say at the same time.

Michael looks a little flushed from running, but his eyes are wide with excitement about something. "Guess what?" he announces.

"I've been elected Mayor?" Dragon guesses. I give him a glance. "What?" he says. "It could happen."

"What's going on?" I ask Michael.

"Remember how my moms got me a camping tent for Christmas but I thought I'd have to wait a couple months until spring to use it?" I nod my head. "Well, they said I can set it up in the basement this weekend and have a sleepover!"

"That's cool," I say.

"So you want to come?" Michael asks.

"To where?"

Michael snorts. "To the sleepover on Friday!"

"A sleepover?" I repeat, thinking about it. I've never been to a sleepover before. But if it's with Michael, it should be fun.

"Sure," I say.

"Great!" Michael replies.

"I can't wait for the sleepover," Dragon muses. "There'll probably be pizza, and treats, and games." It does sound pretty great. Dragon continues, "Also, because we'll be in a different house at nighttime, there might be strange noises, dark hallways, and possibly monsters all around just waiting for new victims to terrorize. Should be interesting."

Strange noises? Dark hallways? Monsters?